D1086133

© Copyright 2022 by Sarah Hazel

Written by Sarah Hazel

Cover & Illustrations by Fatima Zeeshan

ISBN: 979-8-218-10795-6

This book is dedicated to my daughter
Celia.

Remember to always look for joy,
even in the least likely of places!

Based on real life events in
a small New England town.

Shoebert was a seal who lived in the Atlantic Ocean.
He was a rather shy seal and often kept to himself.

One day Shoebert decided to go exploring.

He swam with the current.
Then he swam faster, and
faster, all along the seashore.

He turned into the river to catch a break and have something to eat. "Wow. There are lots of new things over here." Shoebert thought.

So he began following a trail of plentiful food when he discovered a tunnel. "What could this be?" Shoebert asked himself.

Being a brave little seal, Shoebert entered the tunnel brimming with curiosity.

It was very dark. This was unchartered territory for any seal!

"What is this place?" Shoebert wondered. "Maybe a tiny little ocean, just for me?"

Shoebert felt right at home here.
He had plenty of things to eat.
He had the whole pond to himself.
So Shoebert decided to stay!

He was such a spectacle and all of the people from town visited him! Shoebert had created so much excitement and joy!
The people could not believe how a seal could end up in the pond.
"It's impossible!"
the people cried out.

Shoebert started getting very comfortable with his new home. He loved the people and all of the attention. The people around him started to worry a little that he was getting TOO comfortable.

Seals are safer in their natural habitat, the ocean. Not in a pond, surrounded by humans.
The people who loved and cared about Shoebert decided that he needed to go back to his home in the ocean.

They tried to catch him safely,
to bring him back to the ocean.
But Shoebert did not want to be
caught.

One night, while everyone was fast asleep, Shoebert did a funny thing. He climbed out of the pond and waddled across the way to the Police Station nearby.

POLICE STATION

The officers working the night shift were stunned! "Is the seal really turning himself in?" They all thought.

It was sad to see Shoebert go. The town's people wished that he could live in the pond forever. He got to ride in a big truck all the way to the Aquarium! The Aquarium gave him a check up to make sure he was healthy and that it was safe for him to go back into the ocean.

Shoebert made his journey back home, into the Atlantic ocean.

Many people believe that he stays close by the shore. And who knows? Maybe one day Shoebert will come back for a visit !?

THANK YOU

Made in the USA
Middletown, DE
05 January 2023